For Cameron
L.J.

For Peter John
J.C.

Copyright © This Edition 2000
Baby's First Book Club®
Bristol, PA 19007
© 1997 Little Tiger Press
an imprint of Magi Publications, London
Text © 1997 Linda Jennings
Illustrations © 1997 Jane Chapman
All rights reserved • Printed in Belgium
ISBN 1-58048-146-9

PENNY AND PUP

by Linda Jennings

Pictures by Jane Chapman

Baby's First Book Club®

On the first night in her new home,
Penny had whined and howled and scratched
at the door. So her family gave her Pup to be
her friend.

Pup was all squashy and floppy, and he
lived in Penny's basket. She chewed and loved
him to bits.

One day Penny and Pup went out into the garden.
Henry the cat was sitting in the yard.

"Hello, Penny," said Henry. "Where are you going?"

Penny put Pup down and gave him a little lick.

"For a walk," said Penny. "Just Pup and me."

"Can I come, too?" asked Henry.

"Pup only wants *me* for a friend," she said. "Sorry."

And picking Pup up again, she trotted down
the path.

By the back gate Betsy the rabbit was
sitting in her hutch. "Penny!" she cried.
"Come and talk to me. I'm lonesome."

"Pup doesn't want to stop to talk.
We're going for a walk, just Pup and me,"
said Penny. "Sorry."

And off she went, with Pup's long legs
trailing behind her.

On the edge of the lawn sat Matt
the fox cub. "Come and play with me!"
he barked.

"Pup doesn't like playing with foxes.
We're going for a walk, just Pup and me,"
said Penny. "Sorry."

Penny turned her back on Matt
and walked with Pup across the yard
to the garden shed.

Under the shed was a big space.
Penny put Pup down gently and sniffed.
It smelled exciting there, like mice and
old bones.

"Let's go exploring, Pup," said
Penny, and pushing Pup in front
of her, she squeezed her head under
the shed.

Penny tried to follow Pup. She wriggled
and squeezed and squeezed and wriggled,
but she was too big to crawl into the space.
"Pup, Pup!" she called, but of course
Pup said nothing. Penny tried to pull Pup
out again, but she couldn't reach him.
She couldn't even *see* him.

Penny sat down and cried. What would
she do without Pup?
And what would Pup do without *her?*

Matt the fox cub heard her and came
trotting across the yard. "I'll help you,"
he said. But though he wriggled and
squeezed and squeezed and wriggled,
he couldn't reach Pup either.

Henry the cat was sitting on the fence, and he saw Matt trying to rescue Pup. "*I'll* help you," he said. But Henry was a fat cat, and he couldn't even fit his *head* under the shed.

Along bounced Betsy the rabbit.
She was feeling happy because she had
escaped from her hutch.

"*I'll* help you," she said. And since Betsy
was a small rabbit, she was able to wriggle
and squeeze and squeeze and wriggle under
the shed—but Pup wasn't there anymore!

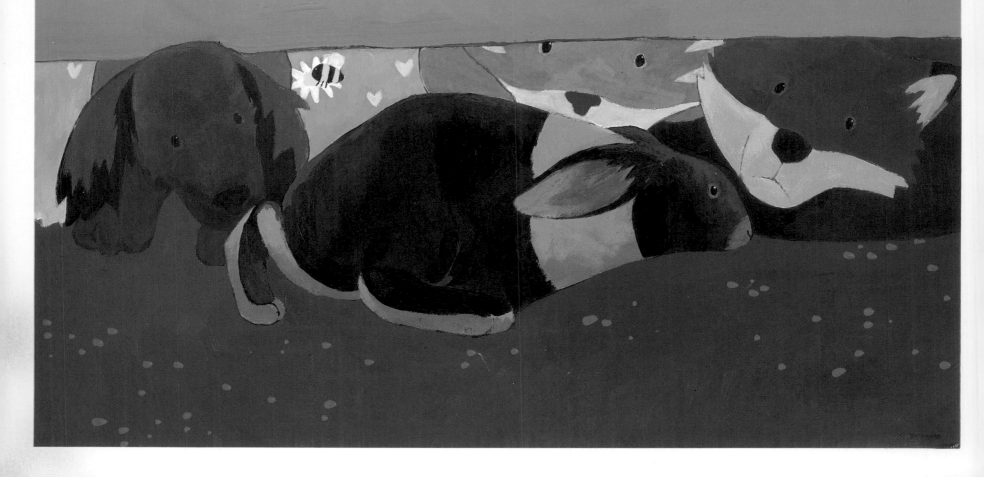

Matt and Henry and Betsy all helped
Penny look for Pup.
     They searched behind the shed.
They searched in the flower beds.
They even searched in the pond,
just in case Pup had fallen in.
     But Pup wasn't anywhere to be found.
And then suddenly . . .

. . . there he was!

Pup was in the hedge. A family of mice had dragged him there, and now they were all curled up together, fast asleep on Pup.

Penny looked at Pup and she looked at the mice. It didn't seem right to disturb them.

"Now you can play with us!" meowed Henry.

"Yes, do!" cried Matt and Betsy together.

"You don't mind, do you, Pup?" asked Penny, but Pup said nothing.

"All right, I *will* play with you," said Penny, and she raced and chased and chased and raced all around the garden with her new friends. Penny was having so much fun that she forgot about Pup.

When it was time to go home, Penny remembered poor old Pup lying in the hedge and went back to fetch him.

The baby mice were still asleep, but their mother was awake. "Pup makes such a cozy bed for my babies," she said. "May we borrow him for a while?"

Pup did seem very happy with the little mice.

"I think Pup would like to
stay with you," Penny said.
"I always thought he needed a
few more friends."